Gravity of Silence

A Journey Beyond Words

Ramnath Sharma

Copyright

About Author

Ramnath Sharma is a poet whose words transcend the ordinary, inviting readers into a world where silence speaks volumes. In Gravity of Silence: A Journey Beyond Words, Sharma masterfully weaves together emotion and insight, creating a collection that captivates and resonates with its profound depth. Sharma's poetry is a journey through the unspoken, revealing the hidden beauty within the quiet moments of life. With a unique blend of lyrical finesse and philosophical depth, Sharma's work promises to leave an indelible mark on the heart and mind of every reader.

Contents

1. The Faceless Girl of my dream

I met a girl in a world unknown,
Where her name's a secret, and her face unshown.
I don't know her laugh, her tears, her voice,
Yet here I am, with no other choice.

I've fallen for her, though she's just a dream,
A shadow in pixels, or so it seems.
My heart, once steady, now skips a beat,
For someone I've never been destined to meet.

In the silence of nights, when I'm all alone,
I miss her deeply, though she's never been known.
My mind has ceased to think with ease,
Only thoughts of her bring me to my knees.

So I grab a pen with trembling hands,
My heart spills words it barely understands.
Every line, every tear-stained page,
Is a cry for the girl who holds my cage.

I write because I can't reach her face,

I write to feel her in this empty space.

My words are broken, my heart laid bare,For a girl unknown, who isn't there.

I don't know her name, I don't know her eyes,

But I feel her presence, like whispered lies.

In every letter, in every verse,

I pour my love, for better or worse.

I miss her so much, it tears me apart,

Yet I've never held her, never felt her heart.

So here I am, with my pen and pain,

Writing for a love that might be in vain

2. To The One I haven't met yet

Under the stars, where dreams softly bloom, He waits for her in the night's quiet gloom. Her laughter, her smile, they haunt his mind, In his dreams, her love is all he can find.

With every breath, he feels her near, Though she's not here, his love's crystal clear. He holds onto hope, as the night gently streams, For she's always with him, in the realm of dreams.

3. An unsaid story

I loved you more than wordscould say, But life pushed us far away.

I had to leave, though it broke my heart, To keep myself from fallingapart.

The dreams we shared now feel so cold,A love story that's left untold.

I walked away to save my soul, But losing you left a gapinghole.

Now every day, I miss you more, With memories that I can't ignore.

We weren't meant to be, it's true,

But that doesn't stop me from missing you

4. The Quiet Night

In the quiet night, I find my soul, Wandering through dreams that make me whole. Stars whisper of loves long lost. Tracing paths where hearts have crossed. Moonlight bathes the world in grace, Revealing tears time can't erase. Yet in the shadows, hope still gleams, A flicker of light in deepest dreams.

5. The girl of my dream

I found a girl I've never met, In dreams and thoughts, she lingers yet. Though I don't know her face or name, Her silent touch has sparked a flame.

When I shared my feelings true, She said she's scared, unsure to0. Her voice was soft, but she withdrew, Now I'm left with just the blue.

A love unknown, a heart that aches, For a girl I've never touched or faced. Confused and lost, we drift apart, A nameless love has won my heart.

6. The dark forest

In the forest, dark and deep, Where shadows and secrets sleep,She hid away from human sight,

A soul untouched by city light.He wandered far from the

busy crowd, Seeking peace where hearts aren't loud, In that wood, their worlds collide,

Two lost souls found side by side.Love bloomed under the moon's glow,

But will it stay or swiftly go? Can love survive the morning's gleam,Or vanish like a fleetingdream?

She asked, "Will you leave or stay?"

He whispered, "I can't walk away."

Yet fear lingered with the dawn's new start,
Would love fade, or bind their hearts?

7. The weave love

In silence, she weaves her love so deep,
Her heart, a secret she quietly keeps,
In every meal, in every tender care,
Her love for him, beyond compare.

She watches him with eyes so kind,
Though her feelings, she tries to hide,
For independence is his chosen creed,
Yet she tends to his every need.

He struts with pride, a veil so tight,
In his heart, she's the guiding light,
Unspoken words, a love so true,
He hides his feelings from view.

She knows his heart is soft inside,
Though he shields it with bravado wide,
In her quiet strength, she stands near,
His silent battles, she holds dear.

And though he may not say the words,
Her love for him is not unheard,
In every unspoken, caring glance,
Her heart sings a silent dance.

So here's to the mother and son,
Their bond, though hidden, brightly spun,
In unvoiced love and care so grand,
They walk together, hand in hand.

8. The forest story that's left untold

In the forest, where shadows wane,
They brewed their secrets in the rain.
The witch, with sightless eyes aglow,
Whispered spells from long ago.
"You won't hurt me," her promise cold,
A tale of ancient power told.
He, a wanderer lost in quest,
Found her heart a darkened nest.
In the tangled woods, where magic blooms,
They danced through the night's dark rooms.
He battled fiercely, torn inside,
Struggling to turn from the tide.
His heart, a storm, fierce and wild,
Begged her to leave, like a frightened child.
In secret storms and midnight's seam,
They weaved through threads of a broken dream.
Her caress, both sharp and sweet,
A haunting touch, a love replete.
In the depths of night, where shadows blend,

Their souls entwined, their hearts unpenned.

A fleeting breath, a tangled kiss,

Love and fear in a bittersweet abyss.

In the morning light, with dawn's first hue,

He faced the forest, the witch's rue.

Their story etched in twilight's mist,

A love both cherished and dismissed.

He left the woods with a heart still torn,

By a love that lived where shadows mourn.

Their tale a whisper on the wind,

A legend of a love that never truly ended

9. In The café blink

In the hum of the café, where laughter flows free,

Our story began, like a whispered plea.

Her friends were laughing, her eyes alight,

But it was her, snatching her phone, that changed the night.

Our gazes met, brief and intense,

A spark ignited, no pretense.

We parted in silence, no words exchanged,

Yet something shifted, our fates rearranged.

On the flyover, where destiny collided,

I saw her again, my heart undecided.

My bike swerved wild, control nearly lost,

Her worried eyes, worth any cost.

The third meeting came, in a rush to our homes,

Our minds distracted, our hearts so alone.

Her bike spun out, pain echoed loud,

A crash, a cry, a soul unbowed.

Scratches and bruises, pain intertwined,

Yet in her eyes, a fire defined.

She stood, her anger, a fierce display,

Beneath it all, a heart that yearned to stay.

She came to my door, bell rang twice,

My mother's worry, a cold, silent vice.

I opened the door, saw her there,

In pain and anger, a moment so rare.

"I'll be back in five," I managed to say,

Her eyes, questioning, but I led the way.

"How did you find me?" I asked with a smile,

"This is your house?" she asked, her voice fragile.

"Yes," I replied, the truth unfolding slow,

She spoke words that made my heart overflow:

"I am the girl you've been wanting to see,"

My heart raced wildly, what a destiny.

I brought her inside, tended her wounds,

In that quiet room, our souls resumed.

Together we went, to a family meeting,

Two hearts entwined, in love's true greeting

In those moments, love's deep song played,

Two hearts united, never to fade.

A "yes" to the future, through joy and strife,

Two souls joined forever, in the dance of life.

10. Echoes in the Silence

Echoes in the Silence

In a crowd, I feel alone,

A heart so heavy, made of stone.

Dreams are close but out of sight,

I wish for someone to make it right.

I want to be seen, to be heard,

But loneliness hangs on every word.

Sadness wraps me, won't let go,

Every glance just makes it grow.

Hearts come near, then break away,

Leaving pieces that can’t stay.

Tears fall down like endless rain,

Why is there no one to ease this pain?

I dream of someone who’ll never leave,

But they all go, like a trick up my sleeve.

Why does love always fade away?

Why do I cry, day after day?

11. The art of noticing

The Art of Noticing

In the quiet of the night, when dreams drift away,

I think of you, though you're far, and I wish you'd stay.

Your smile lights up moments that I can't forget,

But in the silence, my heart feels the regret.

The art of noticing is seeing you clear,

In every small detail, I hold you near.

A laugh, a glance, the way you used to be,

Now just echoes of what used to be.

I see your beauty, though you're out of sight,

In every memory, both day and night.

It's hard to grasp why you're not here,

The pain of missing you is always near.

I notice the warmth that's now gone cold,

In the empty spaces where you used to hold.

The little things that made you bright,

Are now shadows in the deep of night.

So here's to the art of noticing, in my heart's own way,

To the love I had and the words I couldn't say.

Though it's hard to bear, and the tears often flow,

The art of noticing keeps your memory close.

12. I still remember those fake promises

I still remember those fake promises,

Sweet words that were a lie,

Like dried flowers pressed in sadness,

Their beauty left to dry.

You painted dreams in vibrant shades,

But they withered in the light,

Each vow a broken petal,

Lost to the endless night.

I still remember the lies we lived,

Wrapped in a fragile plea,

Every promise you made to me

Was a cruel fantasy.

Now dried flowers on my shelf

Whisper of a love gone cold,

A painful reminder of what we lost,

And the heartache left untold.

13. Why do I write

I often write when words escape,

When speech is locked away,

But mostly, I write when voices flow,

And no one's there to stay.

My thoughts spill onto paper

When conversations cease,

In the quiet of my solitude,

My pen becomes my peace.

For when I can articulate,

Yet no one's there to hear,

I turn my feelings into ink,

In a world that's insincere.

14. The dreamed love

In a world of fleeting glances

and hurried hearts, I yearn for a love that gently imparts. Where ink flows like rivers on

parchment so white, And letters unfurl in the stillness of night.

With kisses that linger on fingertips' grace, We trace tender paths in the softest embrace. We'd lie on the grass, where the

cool breezes play, And dream under stars until dawn's early ray. Our dance would be slow, in the moon's silvery light, A waltz of two souls, wrapped in warmth through the night. In this love, old-fashioned, both gentle and true, I seek the eternal, the timeless with you.

15. The Silent Battle

The Silent Battle

In the quiet of the early morn,
Where dreams and doubts are gently born,
A student rises, weary yet bold,
In a world of pressure, a story unfolds.
Books are stacked like mountains high,
A future glimpsed through a weary eye,
Each page turned, a silent plea,
For strength and wisdom, to simply be.
The struggle's weight, a heavy load,
Through sleepless nights and a lonely road,
Yet within the heart, a flame remains,
Guiding through the shadows and the pains.
In every challenge, a quiet grace,
In every tear, a hopeful trace,
For the battle fought in silence loud,
Will lead to triumph, proud and unbowed

16. Love's Hidden Garden

Love's Hidden Garden

In a garden where the roses bloom,

Two hearts meet in a quiet room,

Among the thorns, where secrets lie,

Love's gentle whispers softly sigh.

Petals fall with each hidden glance,

In the quiet of a secret dance,

Words unspoken, feelings true,

In the heart's garden, love's in view.

Beneath the moon's soft, watchful gaze,

Love grows in delicate ways,

In silence, where the heart takes flight,

Finding solace in the quiet night.

For in the garden of what's concealed,

Love's deepest truths are gently revealed,

In every touch, in every sigh,

Love's hidden garden reaches the sky.

17. The Teacher's Legacy

The Teacher's Legacy

In the classroom where wisdom thrives,

A teacher's legacy silently survives,

Through every lesson, every cheer,

They shape the future, far and near.

Their eyes hold stories of every student's plight,

In the quiet hours of endless night,

Crafting futures with a guiding hand,

In the journey where dreams expand.

The sacrifice is often unseen,

In the classroom's quiet sheen,

Yet in every heart touched, a spark ignites,

Guiding souls through darkened nights.

In every lesson, every shared truth,

The teacher plants seeds of youth,

Their impact, though softly sown,

Becomes the roots of dreams well grown.

18. The Newcomer's Journey

The Newcomer's Journey

In the bustling halls of an unfamiliar place,
A new student searches for a space,
Amongst the crowd, their heart feels small,
A journey begins in the school's grand hall.
Faces blur and voices fade,
In the maze of hallways, hopes cascade,
Loneliness wraps in a cloak so tight,
Yet hope flickers in the dimming light.
Friendships seem a distant shore,
Yet the heart yearns for something more,
In each interaction, a chance to find,
A place where their spirit can unwind.
As days unfold and seasons pass,
The newcomer finds a place at last,
In the laughter and the shared dreams,
Where hope and friendship gently gleams

19. The Burden of Perfection

The Burden of Perfection

In the mirror's gaze, a future bright,
Yet perfection's shadow looms in sight,
The quest for grades, the endless chase,
In a world where standards interlace.
Each test, each score, a measure of worth,
In the quest to prove, to show their girth,
The heart bears the weight of endless demands,
In the pursuit of life's exacting plans.
Yet in the pressure, a light may gleam,
A truth beyond the grades and dream,
For perfection is but a fleeting shade,
In the heart where true strength is made.
The journey's trials, the setbacks faced,
Are not in vain, nor love misplaced,
In every struggle, the heart does grow,
Beyond the perfection it strives to show.

20. Long-Distance Love

Long-Distance Love

Across the miles, where silence speaks,
A love endures, though time may creak,
In messages and calls, feelings share,
A connection woven through the air.
Distance stretches, hearts remain,
Bound by dreams, despite the strain,
Each "goodnight" and "I miss you" sent,
In every whisper, love's intent.
Through screens and voices, tender and true,
Love persists in all it can do,
Though apart, the bond is tight,
In the quiet of the heart's own light.
Time and space may test the soul,
Yet love endures, making us whole,
For though apart, the heart can see,
In each other's dreams, we're free.

21. Friendships Fading

Friendships Fading

Once we walked the same old path,

Shared our dreams, felt the same laugh,

Yet as time flows, we drift apart,

The echoes of laughter, a distant heart.

Friendships, like seasons, come and go,

In the changing winds, we ebb and flow,

Yet the memories linger, warm and bright,

In the corners of our hearts' own light.

Paths may diverge, and lives may change,

Yet the bond remains, never estranged,

In the shared moments and laughter's hue,

The friendship lives in the heart's view.

For though apart, the connection stays,

In the light of past, and the softest rays,

Friendships, though changed, never truly die,

In the heart where they quietly lie.

22. The Echoes of Love Lost

The Echoes of Love Lost

In the pages of a story past,
A love once vivid, now held fast,
Moments of joy, now bittersweet,
In the memories where shadows meet.
Time moves on, the heart does yearn,
For the love that took its turn,
Yet in the echoes of what was true,
A flame of the past remains in view.
The love once held, though now it's gone,
Lives in the heart, a quiet song,
In the silence of what used to be,
A timeless ache, a memory.
Yet in the loss, a lesson learned,
In the heart where hope has burned,
For love once lived, though it may fade,
Leaves a mark that never will trade.

23. The Forgotten Dream

The Forgotten Dream

In the recesses of a crowded mind,

A dream once vivid, now hard to find,

Ambitions lost in daily strife,

A wish to rekindle the fire of life.

Yet within the depths of quiet thought,

A spark remains, though it seems caught,

In the shadows of what might have been,

The dream's whisper, soft and thin.

Through the trials and the endless grind,

The dream endures, though left behind,

In the quiet spaces where hopes reside,

A chance to let the heart's dreams guide.

For dreams, though forgotten, still can rise,

In the stillness of the heart's own skies,

A glimmer of what once was bright,

Can reignite the lost light.

24. The Symphony of Life

The Symphony of Life

In the grand orchestra of time and space,

Life's symphony plays with grace,

Notes of joy, chords of pain,

In the melody where dreams remain.

Each day a movement, each moment a tone,

In the symphony of life, we're never alone,

The highs and lows, the crescendos bold,

In the heart's journey, stories unfold.

Through the struggles and the joys we find,

In every note, a piece of the mind,

The symphony of life, ever grand,

Guides the heart with a gentle hand.

For in the music of the days and nights,

In every harmony, in the softest lights,

Life's symphony plays on, sweet and clear,

In the heart where dreams appear.

25. The Quiet Betrayal

You didn't betray me with grand gestures,
No lies or deceit to be exposed.
It was the quiet slipping away,
The subtle distance nobody knows.

We used to talk, our words like flame,
But now there's only silence to blame.
You drifted far without a sound,
No arguments, no blame passed around.

I try to recall when it began,
The slow unraveling of our plan.
Was it one day, or over years,
That you faded, leaving only fears?

Betrayal doesn't always come with fights,
Sometimes it's hidden in long, lonely nights.
It's in the way you stopped being there,
When I needed you most but you didn't care.

The quiet way you walked away,

Not with anger, not with dismay.

Just with the weight of what you left behind,

A love forgotten, out of mind.

26. The Art of Pretending

I've become a master of pretending,
Of wearing smiles when I want to cry.
I laugh with friends, I play the part,
But inside, I'm silently saying goodbye.

I've learned the art of small talk well,
How to deflect, how to tell
Stories that keep the truth at bay,
So no one sees how much I fray.

It's easier to fake it than to explain
The depths of heartache, the constant pain.
So I put on a show, I act the role,
But every day it takes its toll.

No one knows the mask I wear,
The lies I tell to seem okay.
I keep it hidden, deep and tight,
While losing pieces of me, day by day.

Pretending is an exhausting art,

One that tears my soul apart.

But it's safer than being real,

Safer than revealing how I feel.

27. The Fear of Being Forgotten

I fear one day you'll forget my name,
That all our love will fade like dust.
The memories we made, the dreams we shared,
Will crumble into the depths of mistrust.

What happens when time erases me,
When I'm just a shadow of who I used to be?
Will you remember my voice, my face,
Or will I be lost without a trace?

The fear of being forgotten lingers near,
A haunting presence, always here.
I don't want to vanish from your mind,
Like a chapter left behind.

I gave you all I had to give,
Loved you more than I could live.
But still, I fear the day will come
When my name is no longer sung.

I don't want to be a distant memory,

A photograph lost in history.

I want to stay in your heart and mind,

Not be a love that's left behind.

28. The Loneliness of Waiting

I wait for you in the quiet hours,
When the world has slowed to a crawl.
I wait in the spaces between the days,
Hoping you'll return my call.

Waiting is a kind of loneliness,
A pain that grows without an end.
I count the moments, one by one,
As the silence becomes my closest friend.

I wonder if you think of me,
If you remember the promises we made.
Or am I waiting for a ghost,
For a love that has begun to fade?

Every hour stretches longer still,
A test of patience, a test of will.
But how long can one heart wait?
Before it crumbles beneath the weight.

The loneliness of waiting is deep,

A well of sorrow, a restless sleep.

I wait, though I know the truth inside—

You're never coming back to my side.

29. A Future We Never Knew

We talked about the future once,
About the places we would go.
But now those dreams have turned to dust,
And I wonder if you'll ever know.

The plans we made, the paths we'd walk,
Now feel like distant, forgotten talk.
A future we painted bright and bold,
Now lies forgotten, growing cold.

I wonder what our life could be,
If we had fought, if we had stayed.
Would we have found a way to thrive,
Or would our love have still decayed?

The future is a fleeting thing,
A fragile thread that snaps and sings.
And now I stand at the edge of time,
Wishing for what could have been mine.

The future we never got to see,

Now a dream that's haunting me.

I look ahead but only find

The echoes of what we left behind.

30. The Cost of Loving You

Loving you came with a heavy cost,
A price I didn't know I'd pay.
I gave you all my heart and soul,
But in the end, you walked away.

The nights we spent, the words we shared,
I thought they meant you truly cared.
But love, it seems, is never free,
It takes its toll on hearts like me.

I don't regret the love I gave,
But still, I ache for what I lost.
The dreams we built, the life we planned,
Now just remnants of the cost.

Loving you took everything,
Left me empty, cold, and bare.
Now I'm left with shattered dreams,
And a heart that's worse for wear.

The cost of love is steep indeed,
It drains the soul, it plants the seed
Of doubt, of fear, of deep despair,
Leaving me gasping for air.

31. When Apologies Aren't Enough

You said you were sorry,
But the words fell flat.
An apology can't fix the past,
Can't take back where we're at.

The damage was done, the hurt was real,
And no apology can make me heal.
You think that words can wash away
The scars you left on me that day.

But forgiveness isn't something owed,
It's earned with time, it's something showed.
And though you say you're sorry now,
It doesn't change the why or how.

I needed more than just your regret,
I needed actions, not words you forget.
But all I got were hollow lines,
While the pain remained, etched in time.

Sometimes sorry isn't enough,

When the hurt goes deeper, when life's too tough.

Apologies are words alone,

They cannot mend the broken bone.

32. The Ache of Missing You

I miss you in the quiet hours,
When the world is still and cold.
I miss the way you held my hand,
The love we never told.

I miss the way you smiled at me,
Like I was the only one you'd see.
Now I'm lost in memories,
Wishing for what can never be.

The ache of missing you is deep,
A wound that festers, won't let me sleep.
I try to move on, try to let go,
But missing you is all I know.

Every day feels longer still,
The weight of absence, a bitter pill.
I carry it with me wherever I go,
This constant ache, this painful flow.

33. A Love Left Unsaid

There are things I never told you,
Words I left inside my heart.
Now it's too late to say them,
And it tears me apart.

I loved you in ways I can't describe,
A love so deep, it terrified.
But fear kept me silent, still,
And now I live with the bitter chill.

I wish I could turn back time,
To speak the words, to make you mine.
But love left unsaid is love undone,
A fire extinguished before it's begun.

I hold onto the things I never said,
As they echo loudly inside my head.
The weight of silence is heavy and grim,
A reminder of love that was lost on a whim.

34. The End of All We Were

This is the end of all we were,
The final chapter, the last refrain.
We once were everything, but now
We're nothing but shadows in the rain.

I thought we'd last, I thought we'd fight,
But now we're lost in endless night.
The love we had has come undone,
And all that's left is what we've become.

I want to hold on, to pull you back,
But I know it's too late, the heart attack
Of love's demise is clear as day—
We're over now, we've lost our way.

I'll remember you, I'll remember us,
But the end is here, and all's turned to dust.
This is the end of all we knew,
The final moment where love withdrew

35. The Weight of Words

Words are heavier than we know,
They linger long after they've been said.
I remember every syllable,
The ones you whispered in my head.

You told me I was everything,
A beacon in your darkest night.
But soon your words grew colder still,
And I couldn't see the light.

Each promise cracked beneath the strain,
Your voice turned sharp, became my pain.
I waited for the words to heal,
But instead, they tore, they sealed the deal.

Now silence stands where love once spoke,
The words you gave have left me broke.
I hear them echo through the halls,
Replaying every rise and fall.

I wonder if you meant them all,
Or were they lies just built too tall?
Did you know the weight they'd hold,
The power of words when love turns cold?

Now I carry them like heavy stones,
These words you've left, these hollow tones.
They drag me down, they pull me deep,
Into a darkness where I can't sleep.

I'll never forget what you've said,
Your words now haunt me in my bed.
I wish that I could let them go,
But they're etched in me, and now I know—
Words can kill, as much as heal,
They leave behind a pain that's real.

36. The Silence Between Us

There's a silence now between us,
A gap too wide to cross.
Once we shared our every thought,
But now I grieve the loss.

It used to be so easy,
To talk from dawn till night.
But now your eyes don't meet with mine,
And something's just not right.

We speak in fragments, broken words,
As if we've forgotten how.
I long to bridge the space again,
But don't know where or how.

I miss the laughter, miss the tears,
The way we used to share our fears.
Now silence fills the empty space,
Where once we found a warm embrace.

I wonder if you feel it too,
This distance growing fast.
Or are you content with what we've lost,
Just letting go of what we had?

I've tried to speak, to break the still,
But every word just seems to spill
Into the void between our hearts,
Where conversation fell apart.

So here we sit, so close, so far,
Like strangers under the same star.
The silence between us grows each day,
And I'm afraid it's here to stay.

But if you ever wish to speak,
I'll be here waiting, feeling weak.
For in the silence, all we lose
Is the love we didn't choose.

37. Lost in the Shadows of Yesterday

Yesterday feels so far away,
Yet it clings to me like a ghost.
I find myself trapped in its grasp,
The things I loved and lost the most.

I remember how we used to be,
So full of joy, so wild and free.
But now the past is all I see,
A haunting, cold reality.

Each memory a painful sting,
Of all the joy that time can bring.
But when it fades, what's left behind?
A shadow of the love, entwined.

I can't escape this endless loop,
Of moments gone, a fading truth.
I try to reach beyond the past,

But every step feels like the last.

I wish I could just let it go,
But yesterday won’t let me grow.
It pulls me back, it holds me down,
Till all I wear’s a broken crown.

The life we had, the dreams we knew,
Now slip away, like morning dew.
I want to find tomorrow’s light,
But yesterday holds me too tight.

I’m lost in the shadows, can't break free,
From what we were, from who I used to be.
But I will keep on walking still,
In hopes that one day, I’ll rebuild.

38. The Pain of Goodbye

Goodbye is such a heavy word,
It leaves a scar, it digs in deep.
It's final, and it's cold and sharp,
A pain that never seems to sleep.

When you said goodbye to me,
It felt like everything had died.
The world around me lost its light,
And all I could do was cry.

I never knew a word could hurt
With so much force, with such a sting.
It cuts much deeper than a knife,
And leaves you broken, wondering.

Why did you have to leave me here,
Alone to face the world and fear?
I thought we had a life to build,
But now the dreams we had are stilled.

Goodbye took everything from me,
The love, the hope, the certainty.
It left me cold, it left me bare,
To wander through a life unfair.

I know that time will heal the wound,
But right now all I feel is gloom.
The echoes of your final word
Are the saddest sound I've ever heard.

Goodbye was more than just a phrase,
It took with it our brightest days.
Now all that's left is empty space,
Where once you held me in embrace.

39. When Dreams Collapse

Dreams collapse like fragile things,
Built of glass, on fragile wings.
I had so many dreams with you,
But now they're shattered, through and through.

We talked of futures, of a home,
But now I'm left here all alone.
The life we planned, it fell apart,
And now I'm left with just my heart.

I thought our dreams were strong and bold,
But now they're broken, gone, and cold.
They fell to pieces one by one,
And left me standing, all undone.

The house we'd build, the life we'd share,
Now nothing more than empty air.
The dreams we held so close, so tight,
Now vanish like a fading light.

I gather up the shattered glass,
Of all the dreams that couldn't last.
I try to fix what we had lost,
But broken dreams come at a cost.

How do you build again from dust?
How do you learn again to trust?
When dreams collapse, they leave a scar,
A reminder of how fragile they are.

But still, I dream, despite the pain,
Hoping one day to start again.
For dreams may fall, but they can rise,
And build a future in the skies.

40. The Empty Promises We Made

Promises are easy things,
They flow like water, soft and sweet.
But keeping them is much more hard,
It's where the heart and truth must meet.

We made so many promises,
Of love and life, of dreams come true.
But now I stand in emptiness,
Surrounded by the lies we drew.

You promised me forevermore,
But forever slipped away from shore.
I promised I would never leave,
But even I could not believe.

Each vow we took has turned to dust,
Our words dissolved in fading trust.
The promises we held so dear,
Now feel like whispers I can't hear.

I wonder if you ever meant
The words you said, the time we spent.
Or were they just a fleeting phase,
A moment lost in time's long maze?

Empty promises echo loud,
Like distant thunder in a cloud.
They hold no weight, they bear no truth,
And leave us stranded in our youth.

I wanted to believe in you,
To trust the promises you grew.
But now I know that words alone
Can't build a love or make a home.

41. The Fall of Us

We fell apart so slowly,
I didn't see it happen fast.
I thought we'd stand the test of time,
But now we're just a shadow of the past.

At first, it was just little things,
A missed call, a broken ring.
But soon the gaps grew wide and deep,
Until all we had was lost in sleep.

I tried to hold us up, to fight,
But all my efforts lost their light.
We fell, not with a single blow,
But slowly, surely, down below.

I wish I knew when it began,
When love gave way, when pain began.
But all I know is that we've changed,
And what we were has been estranged.

Now I sit among the ruins here,
Of what we built, of what was dear.
And wonder how we got so far,
From where we thought we'd always are.

The fall of us was quiet, still,
Like snow that covers every hill.
No sound, no fight, just cold decay,
As love slipped silently away.

42. The Fragile Heart

My heart was fragile, like a rose,
Delicate, full of sweet repose.
I gave it freely, held it high,
But you just watched it wilt and die.

I trusted you to hold it dear,
To keep it safe, to keep it near.
But you let it fall, you let it break,
And now I'm left with the pieces to take.

A fragile heart cannot withstand
The careless touch of a cruel hand.
It cracks, it shatters, it bleeds with ease,
It aches in silence, begs for peace.

43. The Endless Wait

I wait for dawn, a fleeting grace,
For light to touch this weary face.
The night seems endless, cold, and deep,
A barren stretch where shadows creep.

I count the hours, the minutes too,
The time it takes for skies to blue.
Each tick of the clock, a heavy weight,
As I endure this endless wait.

I wait for you to find your way,
To bridge the gap, to end the gray.
The silence stretches far and wide,
A desert where my hopes have died.

I dream of words you'll someday say,
To chase these darkened clouds away.
But every moment drags along,
A painful verse of an unsung song.

I see the stars, they shine so bright,
But they can't pierce this endless night.
I yearn for morning, for a sign,
A whisper that your heart is mine.

The dawn will come, I know it's true,
But till it does, I'll wait for you.
In the quiet, in the dark,
I hold a flicker, a tiny spark.

I hope that soon the day will break,
And with it, the promises we'll make.
Till then, I wait, I sit, I sigh,
Underneath this darkened sky.

44. Fading Memories

Memories fade like autumn leaves,
Drifting on the wind, they leave.
Once vivid, now they blur and wane,
Like echoes lost in a distant rain.

I try to hold onto the past,
To grasp the moments that couldn't last.
But they slip through my fingers, thin,
Vanishing where the shadows begin.

The laughter, the tears, the moments shared,
Now seem like whispers, unprepared.
I reach for faces, touch, and grace,
But they dissolve without a trace.

Photographs and old mementos,
Tell a story that now feels hollow.
The feelings once so fresh and true,
Are now like ghosts, a fading hue.

I want to remember every part,
But the past evades my weary heart.
The faces blur, the names grow faint,
And all that's left is a ghostly paint.

The love we had, the dreams we spun,
Are now like shadows, one by one.
I chase the echoes of yesterday,
But they vanish like the break of day.

The past retreats, and I am left,
With only remnants of what's bereft.
I wish I could reclaim the time,
But memories fade like a lost rhyme.

45. The Distant Echo

Your voice was once a comforting sound,
A melody that wrapped me round.
But now it's just a distant echo,
A whisper from the long ago.

I hear it faintly in my dreams,
A soft, elusive, silent scream.
It used to be a guiding star,
Now it's a shadow, lost and far.

I strain to catch the tones you sang,
But all I hear is a distant clang.
The words that once were clear and bright,
Now fade into the dead of night.

I search for traces in the dark,
A lingering note, a fleeting spark.
But all that's left is empty space,
Where your voice once held its place.

The echo lingers, bittersweet,
A reminder of the love we'd meet.
It haunts the silence, fills the void,
A memory that's now destroyed.

I wish I could hear you again,
To end this silence, this deep pain.
But the echoes drift and slowly die,
And I'm left with a muted sky.

In the quiet, your voice is missed,
A distant song, a faded kiss.
I long for sound, for warmth, for light,
But all I have is the empty night.

46. The Fading Touch

Your touch was once my greatest comfort,
A balm for every ache and pain.
But now it's gone, a distant memory,
A softness lost in the heavy rain.

I reach for you in the dark,
But my hands grasp only air.
The warmth that used to fill my heart,
Is now a chill, a cold despair.

Your touch was tender, kind, and true,
It healed me when I felt so blue.
But now it's just a fleeting ghost,
A whisper of what I miss the most.

The way you held me close at night,
And made the world seem so right.
Now feels like a dream I can't retrieve,
A comfort lost, a heart to grieve.

I wish I could relive those days,
To feel your touch, to see your gaze.
But time has turned your warmth to ice,
And left me longing, paying the price.

Your touch was a promise made in skin,
A soft embrace where love begins.
But now it's lost, like morning dew,
Leaving me with just memories of you.

The fading touch is all I know,
A gentle trace where love did flow.
And though I ache for what was real,
I'm left with echoes that I feel.

47. The Lost Promise

Promises were like sacred vows,
A pledge of love, a solemn bound.
But now they lie in disarray,
A promise lost, cast away.

We swore we'd never part,
That we'd stay close, heart to heart.
But now those words are torn apart,
A hollow shell of what we start.

The promises we made with grace,
Now seem like shadows, out of place.
They held a future, bright and clear,
But now they've vanished, disappeared.

I remember when we made them strong,
With hope and love, where we belong.
But time has shown they were a lie,
A fleeting wish that couldn't fly.

I see the remnants of our trust,
Scattered like ashes in the dust.
The future we had planned is gone,
And I am left here, carrying on.

The lost promise weighs me down,
A broken vow, a shattered crown.
I wish we could reclaim the past,
But promises are seldom meant to last.

Now I move through life's embrace,
With echoes of a broken place.
The lost promise is all that's left,
A silent sorrow, deeply bereft.

48. The Shattered Dream

Dreams can be fragile, soft and bright,
Like glass that shatters in the night.
Our dreams were once so full of grace,
Now scattered pieces, lost in space.

We built a world of hope and light,
Of future days, of endless night.
But one small crack, one single break,
Turned dreams to dust, left hearts to ache.

I remember when we dreamed so high,
Our hopes as vast as the endless sky.
But now those dreams lie on the floor,
A shattered vision, nothing more.

We planned our lives with every hope,
But now we're left just trying to cope.
The dreams we had are gone and lost,
A heavy price, a bitter cost.

I try to gather up the shards,

To mend the dreams, to heal the scars.

But every piece is sharp and cold,

A reminder of a future sold.

The shattered dream is all I see,

A broken promise, a memory.

Yet still, I hope, despite the pain,

To find new dreams, to live again.

49. The Cold Goodbye

Goodbye was colder than the frost,
A chill that left me feeling lost.
Your final words, so harsh, so still,
Echoed in me, a winter chill.

I thought we'd end with warmth and grace,
But instead, you left without a trace.
The farewell was a biting breeze,
That stripped away all my ease.

You walked away, no last embrace,
No final touch, no tender face.
Just a word that cut so deep,
A goodbye that made my heart weep.

I tried to understand the why,
But all I felt was the cold sky.
The warmth we shared, now turned to ice,
A love that came with a heavy price.

The cold goodbye is hard to bear,
A freezing wind, a vacant stare.
It's not the end I hoped to see,
But just a chill, a bitter plea.

I wish for warmth, for one last kiss,
To remember how we used to miss.
But all that's left is the cold and gray,
A goodbye that took my heart away.

www.ingramcontent.com/pod-product-compliance
Lightning Source LLC
LaVergne TN
LVHW091223150826
845673LV00003B/984

* 9 7 9 8 2 3 0 1 4 9 1 2 5 *